Defoe Abbott Marx Hardy Melville Machiavelli Montaigne Chesterton Haggard Cooper Emerson Joyce Austen Hugo Eliot Grimm Molière

Stoker Wilde Carroll Christie Maupassant Byron Engels Schiller Smith Kafka Hall

Garnett Goethe Cotton Einstein Fitzgerald Hawthorne Dostoyevsky Kipling Doyle Willis

Baum Henry Nietzsche Turgenev Balzac Crane

Leslie Dumas Flaubert Stockton Vatsyayana Verne Vinci

Burroughs Curtis Tocqueville Whitman Gogol Busch

Homer Widger Tolstoy Thoreau

Darwin Twain Scott Plato Harte

Potter Freud Zola Lawrence Dickens Hesse Burton

Kant Jowett Stevenson

Andersen Voltaire Cervantes Cooke

London Descartes

Poe Aristotle Wells Hale James Hastings Irving

Bunner Shakespeare

Richter da Chambers Benedict Alcott

Doré Dante Chekhov Shaw Wodehouse Pushkin

Swift Newton

tredition

tredition was established in 2006 by Sandra Latusseck and Soenke Schulz. Based in Hamburg, Germany, tredition offers publishing solutions to authors and publishing houses, combined with worldwide distribution of printed and digital book content. tredition is uniquely positioned to enable authors and publishing houses to create books on their own terms and without conventional manufacturing risks.

For more information please visit: www.tredition.com

TREDITION CLASSICS

This book is part of the TREDITION CLASSICS series. The creators of this series are united by passion for literature and driven by the intention of making all public domain books available in printed format again - worldwide. Most TREDITION CLASSICS titles have been out of print and off the bookstore shelves for decades. At tredition we believe that a great book never goes out of style and that its value is eternal. Several mostly non-profit literature projects provide content to tredition. To support their good work, tredition donates a portion of the proceeds from each sold copy. As a reader of a TREDITION CLASSICS book, you support our mission to save many of the amazing works of world literature from oblivion. See all available books at www.tredition.com.

Project Gutenberg

The content for this book has been graciously provided by Project Gutenberg. Project Gutenberg is a non-profit organization founded by Michael Hart in 1971 at the University of Illinois. The mission of Project Gutenberg is simple: To encourage the creation and distribution of eBooks. Project Gutenberg is the first and largest collection of public domain eBooks.

The Disowned

Volume 8

Baron Edward Bulwer Lytton Lytton

Imprint

This book is part of TREDITION CLASSICS

Author: Baron Edward Bulwer Lytton Lytton
Cover design: Buchgut, Berlin – Germany

Publisher: tredition GmbH, Hamburg - Germany
ISBN: 978-3-8424-3083-9

www.tredition.com
www.tredition.de

CHAPTER LXXXII.

Plot on thy little hour, and skein on skein
Weave the vain mesh, in which thy subtle soul
Broods on its venom! Lo! behind, before,
Around thee, like an armament of cloud,
The black Fate labours onward — ANONYMOUS.

The dusk of a winter's evening gathered over a room in Crauford's house in town, only relieved from the closing darkness by an expiring and sullen fire, beside which Mr. Bradley sat, with his feet upon the fender, apparently striving to coax some warmth into the icy palms of his spread hands. Crauford himself was walking up and down the room with a changeful step, and ever and anon glancing his bright, shrewd eye at the partner of his fraud, who, seemingly unconscious of the observation he underwent, appeared to occupy his attention solely with the difficulty of warming his meagre and withered frame.

"Ar'n't you very cold there, sir?" said Bradley, after a long pause, and pushing himself farther into the verge of the dying embers, "may I not ring for some more coals?"

"Hell and the—: I beg your pardon, my good Bradley, but you vex me beyond patience; how can you think of such trifles when our very lives are in so imminent a danger?"

"I beg your pardon, my honoured benefactor, they are indeed in danger!"

"Bradley, we have but one hope,—fidelity to each other. If we persist in the same story, not a tittle can be brought home to us,—not a tittle, my good Bradley; and though our characters may be a little touched, why, what is a character? Shall we eat less, drink less, enjoy less, when we have lost it? Not a whit. No, my friend, we will go abroad: leave it to me to save from the wreck of our fortunes enough to live upon like princes."

"If not like peers, my honoured benefactor."

"'Sdeath!—yes, yes, very good,—he! he! he! if not peers. Well, all happiness is in the senses, and Richard Crauford has as many senses as Viscount Innisdale; but had we been able to protract inquiry another week, Bradley, why, I would have been my Lord, and you Sir John."

"You bear your losses like a hero, sir," said Mr. Bradley. To be sure: there is no loss, man, but life,—none; let us preserve that—and it will be our own fault if we don't—and the devil take all the rest. But, bless me, it grows late, and, at all events, we are safe for some hours; the inquiry won't take place till twelve to-morrow, why should we not feast till twelve to-night? Ring, my good fellow: dinner must be nearly ready."

"Why, honoured sir," said Bradley, "I want to go home to see my wife and arrange my house. Who knows but I may sleep in Newgate to- morrow?"

Crauford, who had been still walking to and fro, stopped abruptly at this speech; and his eye, even through the gloom, shot out a livid and fierce light, before which the timid and humble glance of Mr. Bradley quailed in an instant.

"Go home!—no, my friend, no: I can't part with you tonight, no, not for an instant. I have many lessons to give you. How are we to learn our parts for to-morrow, if we don't rehearse them before-hand? Do you not know that a single blunder may turn what I hope will be a farce into a tragedy? Go home!—pooh! pooh! why, man, I have not seen my wife, nor put my house to rights, and if you do but listen to me I tell you again and again that not a hair of our heads can be touched."

"You know best, honoured sir; I bow to your decision."

"Bravo, honest Brad! and now for dinner. I have the most glorious champagne that ever danced in foam to your lip. No counsellor like the bottle, believe me!"

And the servant entering to announce dinner, Crauford took Bradley's arm, and leaning affectionately upon it, passed through an obsequious and liveried row of domestics to a room blazing with light and plate. A noble fire was the first thing which revived Bradley's spirit; and, as he spread his hands over it before he sat down to the table, he surveyed, with a gleam of gladness upon his thin cheeks, two vases of glittering metal formerly the boast of a king, in which were immersed the sparkling genii of the grape.

Crauford, always a gourmand, ate with unusual appetite, and pressed the wine upon Bradley with an eager hospitality, which soon somewhat clouded the senses of the worthy man. The dinner was removed, the servants retired, and the friends were left alone.

"A pleasant trip to France!" cried Crauford, filling a bumper. "That's the land for hearts like ours. I tell you what, little Brad, we will leave our wives behind us, and take, with a new country and new names, a new lease of life. What will it signify to men making love at Paris what fools say of them in London? Another bumper, honest Brad, — a bumper to the girls! What say you to that, eh?"

"Lord, sir, you are so facetious, so witty! It must be owned that a black eye is a great temptation, — Lira-lira, la-la!" and Mr. Bradley's own eyes rolled joyously.

"Bravo, Brad! — a song, a song! but treason to King Burgundy! Your glass is — "

"Empty, honoured sir, I know it! — Lira-lira la! — but it is easily filled! We who have all our lives been pouring from one vessel into another know how to keep it up to the last!

'Courage then, cries the knight, we may yet be forgiven,
  Or at worst buy the bishop's reversion in heaven;
  Our frequent escapes in this world show how true 't is
  That gold is the only Elixir Salutis.
          Derry down, Derry down.'

'All you who to swindling conveniently creep,
  Ne'er piddle; by thousands the treasury sweep
  Your safety depends on the weight of the sum,
  For no rope was yet made that could tie up a plum.

Derry down, etc.'"

[From a ballad called "The Knight and the Prelate."]

"Bravissimo, little Brad!—you are quite a wit! See what it is to have one's faculties called out. Come, a toast to old England, the land in which no man ever wants a farthing who has wit to steal it,— 'Old England forever!' your rogue is your only true patriot!" and Crauford poured the remainder of the bottle, nearly three parts full, into a beaker, which he pushed to Bradley. That convivial gentleman emptied it at a draught, and, faltering out, "Honest Sir John!—room for my Lady Bradley's carriage," dropped down on the floor insensible.

Crauford rose instantly, satisfied himself that the intoxication was genuine, and giving the lifeless body a kick of contemptuous disgust, left the room, muttering, "The dull ass, did he think it was on his back that I was going to ride off? He! he! he! But stay, let me feel my pulse. Too fast by twenty strokes! One's never sure of the mind if one does not regulate the body to a hair! Drank too much; must take a powder before I start."

Mounting by a back staircase to his bedroom, Crauford unlocked a chest, took out a bundle of clerical clothes, a large shovel hat, and a huge wig. Hastily, but not carelessly, induing himself in these articles of disguise, he then proceeded to stain his fair cheeks with a preparation which soon gave them a swarthy hue. Putting his own clothes in the chest, which he carefully locked (placing the key in his pocket), he next took from a desk on his dressing-table a purse; opening this, he extracted a diamond of great size and immense value, which, years before, in preparation of the event that had now taken place, he had purchased.

His usual sneer curled his lip as he gazed at it. "Now," said he, "is it not strange that this little stone should supply the mighty wants of that grasping thing, man? Who talks of religion, country, wife, children? This petty mineral can purchase them all! Oh, what a bright joy speaks out in your white cheek, my beauty! What are all human charms to yours? Why, by your spell, most magical of talismans, my years may walk, gloating and revelling, through a lane of beauties, till they fall into the grave! Pish! that grave is an ugly thought, — a very, very ugly thought! But come, my sun of hope, I must eclipse you for a while! Type of myself, while you hide, I hide also; and when I once more let you forth to the day, then shine out Richard Crauford, — shine out!" So saying, he sewed the diamond carefully in the folds of his shirt; and, rearranging his dress, took the cooling powder, which he weighed out to a grain, with a scrupulous and untrembling hand; descended the back stairs; opened the door, and found himself in the open street.

The clock struck ten as he entered a hackney-coach and drove to another part of London. "What, so late!" thought he; "I must be at Dover in twelve hours: the vessel sails then. Humph! some danger yet! What a pity that I could not trust that fool! He! he! he! — what will he think tomorrow, when he wakes and finds that only one is destined to swing!"

The hackney-coach stopped, according to his direction, at an inn in the city. Here Crauford asked if a note had been left for Dr. Stapylton. One (written by himself) was given to him.

"Merciful Heaven!" cried the false doctor, as he read it, "my daughter is on a bed of death!"

The landlord's look wore anxiety; the doctor seemed for a moment paralyzed by silent woe. He recovered, shook his head piteously, and ordered a post-chaise and four on to Canterbury without delay.

"It is an ill wind that blows nobody good!" thought the landlord, as he issued the order into the yard.

The chaise was soon out; the doctor entered; off went the post-boys; and Richard Crauford, feeling his diamond, turned his thoughts to safety and to France.

A little, unknown man, who had been sitting at the bar for the last two hours sipping brandy and water, and who from his extreme taciturnity and quiet had been scarcely observed, now rose. "Landlord," said he, "do you know who that gentleman is?"

"Why," quoth Boniface, "the letter to him was directed, 'For the Rev. Dr. Stapylton; will be called for.'"

"Ah," said the little man, yawning, "I shall have a long night's work of it. Have you another chaise and four in the yard?"

"To be sure, sir, to be sure!" cried the landlord in astonishment.

"Out with it, then! Another glass of brandy and water,—a little stronger, no sugar!"

The landlord stared; the barmaid stared; even the head-waiter, a very stately person, stared too.

"Hark ye," said the little man, sipping his brandy and water, "I am a deuced good-natured fellow, so I'll make you a great man to-night; for nothing makes a man so great as being let into a great secret. Did you ever hear of the rich Mr. Crauford?"

"Certainly: who has not?"

"Did you ever see him?"

"No! I can't say I ever did."

"You lie, landlord: you saw him to-night."

"Sir!" cried the landlord, bristling up.

The little man pulled out a brace of pistols, and very quietly began priming them out of a small powder-flask.

The landlord started back; the head-waiter cried "Rape!" and the barmaid "Murder!"

"Who the devil are you, sir?" cried the landlord.

"Mr. Tickletrout! the celebrated officer,—thief-taker, as they call it. Have a care, ma'am, the pistols are loaded. I see the chaise is out; there's the reckoning, landlord."

"O Lord! I'm sure I don't want any reckoning: too great an honour for my poor house to be favoured with your company; but [following the little man to the door] whom did you please to say you were going to catch?"

"Mr. Crauford, alias Dr. Stapylton."

"Lord! Lord! to think of it,—how shocking! What has he done?"

"Swindled, I believe."

"My eyes! And why, sir, did not you catch him when he was in the bar?"

"Because then I should not have got paid for my journey to Dover. Shut the door, boy; first stage on to Canterbury." And, drawing a woollen nightcap over his ears, Mr. Tickletrout resigned himself to his nocturnal excursion.

On the very day on which the patent for his peerage was to have been made out, on the very day on which he had afterwards calculated on reaching Paris, on that very day was Mr. Richard Crauford lodged in Newgate, fully committed for a trial of life and death.

CHAPTER LXXXIII.

There, if, O gentle love! I read aright
The utterance that sealed thy sacred bond,
'T was listening to those accents of delight
She hid upon his breast those eyes, beyond
Expression's power to paint, all languishingly fond. —
CAMPBELL.

"And you will positively leave us for London," said Lady Flora, tenderly, "and to-morrow too!" This was said to one who under the name of Clarence Linden has played the principal part in our drama, and whom now, by the death of his brother succeeding to the honours of his house, we present to our reader as Clinton L'Estrange, Earl of Ulswater.

They were alone in the memorable pavilion; and though it was winter the sun shone cheerily into the apartment; and through the door, which was left partly open, the evergreens, contrasting with the leafless boughs of the oak and beech, could be just descried, furnishing the lover with some meet simile of love, and deceiving the eyes of those willing to be deceived with a resemblance to the departed summer. The unusual mildness of the day seemed to operate genially upon the birds, — those children of light and song; and they grouped blithely beneath the window and round the door, where the hand of the kind young spirit of the place had so often ministered to their wants. Every now and then, too, you might hear the shrill glad note of the blackbird keeping measure to his swift and low flight, and sometimes a vagrant hare from the neighbouring preserves sauntered fearlessly by the half-shut door, secure, from long experience, of an asylum in the vicinity of one who had drawn from the breast of Nature a tenderness and love for all its offspring.

Her lover sat at Flora's feet; and, looking upward, seemed to seek out the fond and melting eyes which, too conscious of their secret, turned bashfully from his gaze. He had drawn her arm over his shoulder; and clasping that small and snowy hand, which, long coveted with a miser's desire, was at length won, he pressed upon it a thousand kisses, sweeter beguilers of time than even words. All had been long explained; the space between their hearts annihilated; doubt, anxiety, misconstruction, those clouds of love, had passed away, and left not a wreck to obscure its heaven.

"And you will leave us to-morrow; must it be to-morrow?"

"Ah! Flora, it must; but see, I have your lock of hair — your beautiful, dark hair — to kiss, when I am away from you, and I shall have your letters, dearest, — a letter every day; and oh! more than all, I shall have the hope, the certainty, that when we meet again, you will be mine forever."

"And I, too, must, by seeing it in your handwriting, learn to reconcile myself to your new name. Ah! I wish you had been still Clarence, — only Clarence. Wealth, rank, power, — what are all these but rivals to poor Flora?"

Lady Flora sighed, and the next moment blushed; and, what with the sigh and the blush, Clarence's lips wandered from the hands to the cheek, and thence to a mouth on which the west wind seemed to have left the sweets of a thousand summers.

CHAPTER LXXXIV.

A Hounsditch man, one of the devil's near kinsmen, — a broker. —
Every
Man in His Humour.

We have here discovered the most dangerous piece of lechery that ever was known in the commonwealth. — Much Ado about Nothing.

It was an evening of mingled rain and wind, the hour about nine, when Mr. Morris Brown, under the shelter of that admirable umbrella of sea- green silk, to which we have before had the honour to summon the attention of our readers, was, after a day of business, plodding homeward his weary way. The obscure streets through which his course was bent were at no time very thickly thronged, and at the present hour the inclemency of the night rendered them utterly deserted. It is true that now and then a solitary female, holding up, with one hand, garments already piteously bedraggled, and with the other thrusting her umbrella in the very teeth of the hostile winds, might be seen crossing the intersected streets, and vanishing amid the subterranean recesses of some kitchen area, or tramping onward amidst the mazes of the metropolitan labyrinth, till, like the cuckoo, "heard," but no longer "seen," the echo of her retreating pattens made a dying music to the reluctant ear; or indeed, at intervals of unfrequent occurrence, a hackney vehicle jolted, rumbling, bumping over the uneven stones, as if groaning forth its gratitude to the elements for which it was indebted for its fare. Sometimes also a chivalrous gallant of the feline species ventured its delicate paws upon the streaming pavement, and shook, with a small but dismal cry, the raindrops from the pyramidal roofs of its tender ears.

But, save these occasional infringements on its empire, solitude, dark, comfortless, and unrelieved, fell around the creaking footsteps of Mr. Morris Brown. "I wish," soliloquized the worthy broker, "that I had been able advantageously to dispose of this cursed umbrella of the late Lady Waddilove; it is very little calculated for any but a single lady of slender shape, and though it certainly keeps the rain off my hat, it only sends it with a double dripping upon my shoulders. Pish, deuce take the umbrella! I shall catch my death of cold."

These complaints of an affliction that was assuredly sufficient to irritate the naturally sweet temper of Mr. Brown, only ceased as that industrious personage paused at the corner of the street, for the purpose of selecting the driest path through which to effect the miserable act of crossing to the opposite side. Occupied in stretching his neck over the kennel, in order to take the fullest survey of its topography which the scanty and agitated lamps would allow, the unhappy wanderer, lowering his umbrella, suffered a cross and violent gust of wind to rush, as if on purpose, against the interior. The rapidity with which this was done, and the sudden impetus, which gave to the inflated silk the force of a balloon, happening to occur exactly at the moment Mr. Brown was stooping with such wistful anxiety over the pavement, that gentleman, to his inexpressible dismay, was absolutely lifted, as it were, from his present footing, and immersed in a running rivulet of liquid mire, which flowed immediately below the pavement. Nor was this all: for the wind, finding itself somewhat imprisoned in the narrow receptacle it had thus abruptly entered, made so strenuous an exertion to extricate itself, that it turned Lady Waddilove's memorable relic utterly inside out; so that when Mr. Brown, aghast at the calamity of his immersion, lifted his eyes to heaven, with a devotion that had in it more of expostulation than submission, he beheld, by the melancholy lamps, the apparition of his umbrella,—the exact opposite to its legitimate conformation, and seeming, with its lengthy stick and inverted summit, the actual and absolute resemblance of a gigantic wineglass.

"Now," said Mr. Brown, with that ironical bitterness so common to intense despair, "now, that's what I call pleasant."

As if the elements were guided and set on by all the departed souls of those whom Mr. Brown had at any time overreached in his profession, scarcely had the afflicted broker uttered this brief sentence, before a discharge of rain, tenfold more heavy than any which had yet fallen, tumbled down in literal torrents upon the defenceless head of the itinerant.

"This won't do," said Mr. Brown, plucking up courage and splashing out of the little rivulet once more into terra firma, "this won't do: I must find a shelter somewhere. Dear, dear, how the wet runs down me! I am for all the world like the famous dripping well in Derbyshire. What a beast of an umbrella! I'll never buy one again of an old lady: hang me if I do."

As the miserable Morris uttered these sentences, which gushed out, one by one, in a broken stream of complaint, he looked round and round — before, behind, beside — for some temporary protection or retreat. In vain: the uncertainty of the light only allowed him to discover houses in which no portico extended its friendly shelter, and where even the doors seemed divested of the narrow ledge wherewith they are, in more civilized quarters, ordinarily crowned.

"I shall certainly have the rheumatism all this winter," said Mr. Brown, hurrying onward as fast as he was able. Just then, glancing desperately down a narrow lane, which crossed his path, he perceived the scaffolding of a house in which repair or alteration had been at work. A ray of hope flashed across him; he redoubled his speed, and, entering the welcome haven, found himself entirely protected from the storm. The extent of the scaffolding was, indeed, rather considerable; and though the extreme narrowness of the lane and the increasing gloom of the night left Mr. Brown in almost total darkness, so that he could not perceive the exact peculiarities of his situation, yet he was perfectly satisfied with the shelter he had obtained; and after shaking the rain from his hat, squeezing his coat sleeves and lappets, satisfying himself that it was only about the shoulders that he was thoroughly wetted, and thrusting two pocket-handkerchiefs between his shirt and his skin, as preventives to the dreaded rheumatism, Mr. Brown leaned luxuriously back against the wall in the farthest corner of his retreat, and busied himself with endeavouring to restore his insulted umbrella to its original utility of shape.

Our wanderer had been about three minutes in this situation; when he heard the voices of two men, who were hastening along the lane.

"But do stop," said one; and these were the first words distinctly audible to the ear of Mr. Brown, "do stop, the rain can't last much longer, and we have a long way yet to go."

"No, no," said the other, in a voice more imperious than the first, which was evidently plebeian and somewhat foreign in its tone, "no, we have no time. What signify the inclemencies of weather to men feeding upon an inward and burning thought, and made, by the workings of the mind, almost callous to the contingencies of the frame?"

"Nay, my very good friend," said the first speaker, with positive though not disrespectful earnestness, "that may be all very fine for you, who have a constitution like a horse; but I am quite a—what call you it—an invalid, eh? and have a devilish cough ever since I have been in this d—d country; beg your pardon, no offence to it; so I shall just step under cover of this scaffolding for a few minutes, and if you like the rain so much, my very good friend, why, there is plenty of room in the lane to—(ugh! ugh! ugh!) to enjoy it."

As the speaker ended, the dim light, just faintly glimmering at the entrance of the friendly shelter, was obscured by his shadow, and presently afterwards his companion, joining him, said,—

"Well, if it must be so; but how can you be fit to brave all the perils of our scheme, when you shrink, like a palsied crone, from the sprinkling of a few water-drops?"

"A few water-drops, my very good friend," answered the other, "a few— what call you them, ay, water-falls rather; (ugh! ugh!) but let me tell you, my brother citizen, that a man may not like to get his skin wet with waters and would yet thrust his arm up to the very elbow in blood! (ugh! ugh!)"

"The devil!" mentally ejaculated Mr. Brown, who at the word "scheme" had advanced one step from his retreat, but who now at the last words of the intruder drew back as gently as a snail into his shell; and although his person was far too much enveloped in shade to run the least chance of detection, yet the honest broker began to feel a little tremor vibrate along the chords of his thrilling frame, and a new anathema against the fatal umbrella rise to his lips.

"Ah!" quoth the second, "I trust that it may be so; but, to return to our project, are you quite sure that these two identical ministers are in the regular habit of walking homeward from that Parliament which their despotism has so degraded?"

"Sure? ay, that I am; Davidson swears to it!"

"And you are also sure of their persons, so that, even in the dusk, you can recognize them? for you know I have never seen them."

"Sure as fivepence!" returned the first speaker, to whose mind the lives of the persons referred to were of considerably less value than the sum elegantly specified in his metaphorical reply.

"Then," said the other, with a deep, stern determination of tone, "then shall this hand, by which one of the proudest of our oppressors has already fallen, be made a still worthier instrument of the wrath of Heaven!"

"You are a d—d pretty shot, I believe," quoth the first speaker, as indifferently as if he were praising the address of a Norfolk squire.

"Never did my eye misguide me, or my aim swerve a hair's-breadth from its target! I thought once, when I learned the art as a boy, that in battle, rather than in the execution of a single criminal, that skill would avail me."

"Well, we shall have a glorious opportunity to-morrow night!" answered the first speaker; "that is, if it does not rain so infernally as it does this night; but we shall have a watch of many hours, I dare say."

"That matters but little," replied the other conspirator; "nor even if, night after night, the same vigil is renewed and baffled, so that it bring its reward at last."

"Right," quoth the first; I long to be at it!—ugh! ugh! ugh!—what a confounded cough I have! it will be my death soon, I'm thinking."

"If so," said the other, with a solemnity which seemed ludicrously horrible, from the strange contrast of the words and object, "die at least with the sanctity of a brave and noble deed upon your conscience and your name!"

"Ugh! ugh!—I am but a man of colour, but I am a patriot, for all that, my good friend! See, the violence of the rain has ceased; we will proceed;" and with these words the worthy pair left the place to darkness and Mr. Brown.

"O Lord!" said the latter, stepping forth, and throwing, as it were, in that exclamation, a whole weight of suffocating emotion from his chest, "what bloody miscreants! Murder his Majesty's ministers!—'shoot them like pigeons!'—'d—d pretty shot!' indeed. O Lord! what would the late Lady Waddilove, who always hated even the Whigs so cordially, say, if she were alive? But how providential that I should have been here! Who knows but I may save the lives of the whole administration, and get a pension or a little place in the post-office? I'll go to the prime minister directly,—this very minute! Pish! ar'n't you right now, you cursed thing?" upbraiding the umbrella, which, half-right and half-wrong, seemed endued with an instinctive obstinacy for the sole purpose of tormenting its owner.

However, losing this petty affliction in the greatness of his present determination, Mr. Brown issued out of his lair, and hastened to put his benevolent and loyal intentions into effect.

CHAPTER LXXXV.

When laurelled ruffians die, the Heaven and Earth,
And the deep Air give warning. Shall the good
Perish and not a sign? — ANONYMOUS.

It was the evening after the event recorded in our last chapter: all was hushed and dark in the room where Mordaunt sat alone; the low and falling embers burned dull in the grate, and through the unclosed windows the high stars rode pale and wan in their career. The room, situated at the back of the house, looked over a small garden, where the sickly and hoar shrubs, overshadowed by a few wintry poplars and grim firs, saddened in the dense atmosphere of fog and smoke, which broods over our island city. An air of gloom hung comfortless and chilling over the whole scene externally and within. The room itself was large and old, and its far extremities, mantled as they were with dusk and shadow, impressed upon the mind that involuntary and vague sensation, not altogether unmixed with awe, which the eye, resting upon a view that it can but dimly and confusedly define, so frequently communicates to the heart. There was a strange oppression at Mordaunt's breast with which he in vain endeavoured to contend. Ever and anon, an icy but passing chill, like the shivers of a fever, shot through his veins, and a wild and unearthly and objectless awe stirred through his hair, and his eyes filled with a glassy and cold dew, and sought, as by a self-impulse, the shadowy and unpenetrated places around, which momently grew darker and darker. Little addicted by his peculiar habits to an over-indulgence of the imagination, and still less accustomed to those absolute conquests of the physical frame over the mental, which seem the usual sources of that feeling we call presentiment, Mordaunt rose, and walking to and fro along the room, endeavoured by the exercise to restore to his veins their wonted and healthful circulation. It was past the hour in which his daughter retired to rest: but he was often accustomed to steal up to her chamber, and watch her in her young slumbers; and he felt this night a more than usual desire to perform that office of love; so he left the room and ascended the stairs. It was a large old house that he tenanted. The staircase was broad, and lighted from above by a glass dome; and as he slowly ascended, and the stars gleamed down still and ghastly upon his steps, he fancied — but he knew not why — that there was an omen in their gleam. He entered the young Isabel's chamber: there was a light burning within; he stole to her bed, and putting aside the curtain, felt, as he looked upon her peaceful and pure beauty, a cheering warmth gather round his heart. How lovely is the sleep of childhood! What worlds of sweet, yet not utterly sweet, associations, does it not mingle with the envy of our gaze! What thoughts and hopes and cares and forebodings does it not excite! There lie in that yet ungrieved and unsullied heart what unnumbered sources of emotion! what deep fountains of passion and woe! Alas! whatever be its earlier triumphs, the victim must fall at last! As the hart which the jackals pursue, the moment its race is begun the human prey is foredoomed for destruction, not by the single sorrow, but the thousand cares: it may baffle one race of pursuers, but a new succeeds; as fast as some drop off exhausted, others spring up to renew and to perpetuate the chase; and the fated, though flying victim never escapes but in death. There was a faint smile upon his daughter's lip, as Mordaunt bent down to kiss it; the dark lash rested on the snowy lid — ah, that tears had no well beneath its surface! — - and her breath stole from her rich lips with so regular and calm a motion that, like the "forest leaves," it "seemed stirred with prayer!" [And yet the forest leaves seem stirred with prayer. — BYRON.] One arm lay over the coverlet, the other pillowed her head, in the unrivalled grace of infancy.

Mordaunt stooped once more, for his heart filled as he gazed upon his child, to kiss her cheek again, and to mingle a blessing with the kiss. When he rose, upon that fair smooth face there was one bright and glistening drop; and Isabel stirred in sleep, and, as if suddenly vexed by some painful dream, she sighed deeply as she stirred. It was the last time that the cheek of the young and predestined orphan was ever pressed by a father's kiss or moistened by a father's tear! He left the room silently; no sooner had he left it, than, as if without the precincts of some charmed and preserving circle, the chill and presentiment at his heart returned. There is a feeling which perhaps all have in a momentary hypochondria felt at times: it is a strong and shuddering impression which Coleridge has embodied in his own dark and supernatural verse, that something not of earth is behind us; that if we turned our gaze backward we should behold that which would make the heart as a bolt of ice, and the eye shrivel and parch within its socket. And so intense is the fancy that when we turn, and all is void, from that very void we could shape a spectre, as fearful as the image our terror had foredrawn. Somewhat such feeling had Mordaunt now, as his steps sounded hollow and echoless on the stairs, and the stars filled the air around him with their shadowy and solemn presence. Breaking by a violent effort from a spell of which he felt that a frame somewhat overtasked of late was the real enchanter, he turned once more into the room which he had left to visit Isabel. He had pledged his personal attendance at an important motion in the House of Commons for that night, and some political papers were left upon his table which he had promised to give to one of the members of his party. He entered the room, purposing to stay only a minute; an hour passed before he left it: and his servant afterwards observed that, on giving him some orders as he passed through the hall to the carriage, his cheek was as white as marble, and that his step, usually so haughty and firm, reeled and trembled like a fainting man's. Dark and inexplicable Fate! weaver of wild contrasts, demon of this hoary and old world, that movest through it, as a spirit moveth over the waters, filling the depths of things with a solemn mystery and an everlasting change! Thou sweepest over our graves, and Joy is born from the ashes: thou sweepest over Joy, and lo, it is a grave! Engine and tool of the Almighty, whose years cannot fade, thou changest the earth as a garment, and as a vesture it is changed; thou makest it one vast sepulchre and womb united, swallowing and creating life! and reproducing, over and over, from age to age, from the birth of creation to the creation's doom, the same dust and atoms which were our fathers, and which are the sole heirlooms that through countless generations they bequeath and perpetuate to their sons.

CHAPTER LXXXVI.

Methinks, before the issue of our fate,
A spirit moves within us, and impels
The passion of a prophet to our lips. — ANONYMOUS.

O vitae Philosophia dux, virtutis indagatrix!-CICERO.
["O Philosophy, conductress of life, searcher after virtue!"]

Upon leaving the House of Commons, Mordaunt was accosted by Lord Ulswater, who had just taken his seat in the Upper House. Whatever abstraction or whatever weakness Mordaunt might have manifested before he had left his home, he had now entirely conquered both; and it was with his usual collected address that he replied to Lord Ulswater's salutations, and congratulated him on his change of name and accession of honours.

It was a night of uncommon calm and beauty; and, although the moon was not visible, the frosty and clear sky, "clad in the lustre of its thousand stars," [Marlowe] seemed scarcely to mourn either the hallowing light or the breathing poesy of her presence; and when Lord Ulswater proposed that Mordaunt should dismiss his carriage, and that they should walk home, Algernon consented not unwillingly to the proposal. He felt, indeed, an unwonted relief in companionship; and the still air and the deep heavens seemed to woo him from more unwelcome thoughts, as with a softening and a sister's love.

"Let us, before we return home," said Lord Ulswater, "stroll for a few moments towards the bridge: I love looking at the river on a night like this"

Whoever inquires into human circumstances will be struck to find how invariably a latent current of fatality appears to pervade them. It is the turn of the atom in the scale which makes our safety or our peril, our glory or our shame, raises us to the throne or sinks us to the grave. A secret voice at Mordaunt's heart prompted him to dissent from this proposal, trifling as it seemed and welcome as it was to his present and peculiar mood: he resisted the voice, — the moment passed away, and the last seal was set upon his doom; they moved onward towards the bridge. At first both were silent, for Lord Ulswater used the ordinary privilege of a lover and was absent and absorbed, and his companion was never the first to break a taciturnity natural to his habits. At last Lord Ulswater said, "I rejoice that you are now in the sphere of action most likely to display your talents: you have not spoken yet, I think; indeed, there has been no fitting opportunity, but you will soon, I trust."

"I know not," said Mordaunt, with a melancholy smile, "whether you judge rightly in thinking the sphere of political exertion the one most calculated for me; but I feel at my heart a foreboding that my planet is not fated to shine in any earthly sphere. Sorrow and misfortune have dimmed it in its birth, and now it is waning towards its decline."

"Its decline!" repeated his companion, "no, rather its meridian. You are in the vigor of your years, the noon of your prosperity, the height of your intellect and knowledge; you require only an effort to add to these blessings the most lasting of all, — Fame!"

"Well," said Mordaunt, and a momentary light flashed over his countenance, "the effort will be made. I do not pretend not to have felt ambition. No man should make it his boast, for it often gives to our frail and earth-bound virtue both its weapon and its wings; but when the soil is exhausted its produce fails; and when we have forced our hearts to too great an abundance, whether it be of flowers that perish or of grain that endures, the seeds of after hope bring forth but a languid and scanty harvest. My earliest idol was ambition; but then came others, love and knowledge, and afterwards the desire to bless. That desire you may term ambition: but we will suppose them separate passions; for by the latter I would signify the thirst for glory, either in evil or in good; and the former teaches us, though by little and little, to gain its object, no less in secrecy than for applause; and Wisdom, which opens to us a world, vast, but hidden from the crowd, establishes also over that world an arbiter of its own, so that its disciples grow proud, and, communing with their own hearts, care for no louder judgment than the still voice within. It is thus that indifference not to the welfare but to the report of others grows over us; and often, while we are the most ardent in their cause, we are the least anxious for their esteem."

"And yet," said Lord Ulswater, "I have thought the passion for esteem is the best guarantee for deserving it."

"Nor without justice: other passions may supply its place, and produce the same effects; but the love of true glory is the most legitimate agent of extensive good, and you do right to worship and enshrine it. For me it is dead: it Survived—ay, the truth shall out!—poverty, want, disappointment, baffled aspirations,—all, all, but the deadness, the lethargy of regret when no one was left upon this altered earth to animate its efforts, to smile upon its success, then the last spark quivered and died; and—and—but forgive me—on this subject I am not often wont to wander. I would say that ambition is for me no more; not so are its effects: but the hope of serving that race whom I have loved as brothers, but who have never known me,—who, by the exterior" (and here something bitter mingled with his voice), "pass sentence upon the heart; in whose eyes I am only the cold, the wayward, the haughty, the morose,—the hope of serving them is to me, now, a far stronger passion than ambition was heretofore; and whatever for that end the love of fame would have dictated, the love of mankind will teach me still more ardently to perform."

They were now upon the bridge. Pausing, they leaned over, and looked along the scene before them. Dark and hushed, the river flowed sullenly on, save where the reflected stars made a tremulous and broken beam on the black surface of the water, or the lights of the vast City, which lay in shadow on its banks, scattered at capricious intervals a pale but unpiercing wanness rather than lustre along the tide, or save where the stillness was occasionally broken by the faint oar of the boatman or the call of his rude voice, mellowed almost into music by distance and the element.

But behind them, as they leaned, the feet of passengers on the great thoroughfare passed not oft,—but quick; and that sound, the commonest of earth's, made rarer and rarer by the advancing night, contrasted rather than destroyed the quiet of the heaven and the solemnity of the silent stars.

"It is an old but a just comparison," said Mordaunt's companion, "which has likened life to a river such as we now survey, gliding alternately in light or in darkness, in sunshine or in storm, to that great ocean in which all waters meet."

"If," said Algernon, with his usual thoughtful and pensive smile, "we may be allowed to vary that simile, I would, separating the universal and eternal course of Destiny from the fleeting generations of human life, compare the river before us to that course, and not it, but the city scattered on its banks, to the varieties and mutability of life. There (in the latter) crowded together in the great chaos of social union, we herd in the night of ages, flinging the little lustre of our dim lights over the sullen tide which rolls beside us, — seeing the tremulous ray glitter on the surface, only to show us how profound is the gloom which it cannot break, and the depths which it is too faint to pierce. There Crime stalks, and Woe hushes her moan, and Poverty couches, and Wealth riots, — and Death, in all and each, is at his silent work. But the stream of Fate, unconscious of our changes and decay, glides on to its engulfing bourne; and, while it mirrors the faintest smile or the lightest frown of heaven, beholds, without a change upon its surface, the generations of earth perish, and be renewed, along its banks!"

There was a pause; and by an involuntary and natural impulse, they turned from the waves beneath to the heaven which, in its breathing contrast, spread all eloquently, yet hushed, above. They looked upon the living and intense stars, and felt palpably at their hearts that spell — wild, but mute — which nothing on or of earth can inspire; that pining of the imprisoned soul, that longing after the immortality on high, which is perhaps no imaginary type of the immortality ourselves are heirs to.

"It is on such nights as these," said Mordaunt, who first broke the silence, but with a low and soft voice, "that we are tempted to believe that in Plato's divine fancy there is as divine a truth; that 'our souls are indeed of the same essence as the stars,' and that the mysterious yearning, the impatient wish which swells and soars within us to mingle with their glory, is but the instinctive and natural longing to re-unite the divided portion of an immortal spirit, stored in these cells of clay, with the original lustre of the heavenly and burning whole!"

And hence then," said his companion, pursuing the idea, "might we also believe in that wondrous and wild influence which the stars have been fabled to exercise over our fate; hence might we shape a visionary clew to their imagined power over our birth, our destinies, and our death."

"Perhaps," rejoined Mordaunt, and Lord Ulswater has since said that his countenance as he spoke wore an awful and strange aspect, which lived long and long afterwards in the memory of his companion, "perhaps they are tokens and signs between the soul and the things of Heaven which do not wholly shame the doctrine of him [Socrates, who taught the belief in omens.] from whose bright wells Plato drew (while he coloured with his own gorgeous errors) the waters of his sublime lore." As Mordaunt thus spoke, his voice changed: he paused abruptly, and, pointing to a distant quarter of the heavens, said, —

"Look yonder; do you see, in the far horizon, one large and solitary star, that, at this very moment, seems to wax pale and paler, as my hand points to it?"

"I see it; it shrinks and soars, while we gaze into the farther depths of heaven, as if it were seeking to rise to some higher orbit."

"And do you see," rejoined Mordaunt, "yon fleecy but dusky cloud which sweeps slowly along the sky towards it? What shape does that cloud wear to your eyes?"

"It seems to me," answered Lord Ulswater, "to assume the exact semblance of a funeral procession: the human shape appears to me as distinctly moulded in the thin vapours as in ourselves; nor would it perhaps ask too great indulgence from our fancy to image amongst the darker forms in the centre of the cloud one bearing the very appearance of a bier, — the plume, and the caparison, and the steeds, and the mourners! Still, as I look, the likeness seems to me to increase!"

"Strange!" said Mordaunt, musingly, "how strange is this thing which we call the mind! Strange that the dreams and superstitions of childhood should cling to it with so inseparable and fond a strength! I remember, years since, that I was affected even as I am now, to a degree which wiser men might shrink to confess, upon gazing on a cloud exactly similar to that which at this instant we behold. But see: that cloud has passed over the star; and now, as it rolls away, look, the star itself has vanished into the heavens."

"But I fear," answered Lord Ulswater, with a slight smile, "that we can deduce no omen either from the cloud or the star: would, indeed, that Nature were more visibly knit with our individual existence! Would that in the heavens there were a book, and in the waves a voice, and on the earth a token of the mysteries and enigmas of our fate!"

"And yet," said Mordaunt, slowly, as his mind gradually rose from its dream-like oppression to its wonted and healthful tone, "yet, in truth, we want neither sign nor omen from other worlds to teach us all that it is the end of existence to fulfil in this; and that seems to me a far less exalted wisdom which enables us to solve the riddles, than that which elevates us above the chances, of the future."

"But can we be placed above those chances;—can we become independent of that fate to which the ancients taught that even their deities were submitted?"

"Let us not so wrong the ancients," answered Mordaunt; "their poets taught it, not their philosophers. Would not virtue be a dream, a mockery indeed, if it were, like the herb of the field, a thing of blight and change, of withering and renewal, a minion of the sunbeam and the cloud? Shall calamity deject it? Shall prosperity pollute? then let it not be the object of our aspiration, but the byword of our contempt. No: let us rather believe, with the great of old, that when it is based on wisdom, it is throned above change and chance! throned above the things of a petty and sordid world! throned above the Olympus of the heathen! throned above the Stars which fade, and the Moon which waneth in her course! Shall we believe less of the divinity of Virtue than an Athenian Sage? Shall we, to whose eyes have been revealed without a cloud the blaze and the glory of Heaven, make Virtue a slave to those chains of earth which the Pagan subjected to her feet? But if by her we can trample on the ills of life, are we not a hundredfold more by her the vanquishers of death? All creation lies before us: shall we cling to a grain of dust? All immortality is our heritage: shall we gasp and sicken for a moment's breath? What if we perish within an hour? — what if already the black cloud lowers over us? — what if from our hopes and projects, and the fresh woven ties which we have knit around our life, we are abruptly torn? — shall we be the creatures or the conquerors of fate? Shall we be the exiled from a home, or the escaped from a dungeon? Are we not as birds which look into the Great Air only through a barred cage? Shall we shrink and mourn when the cage is shattered, and all space spreads around us, — our element and our empire? No; it was not for this that, in an elder day, Virtue and Valour received but a common name! The soul, into which that Spirit has breathed its glory, is not only above Fate, — it profits by her assaults! Attempt to weaken it, and you nerve it with a new strength; to wound it, and you render it more invulnerable; to destroy it, and you make it immortal! This, indeed, is the Sovereign whose realm every calamity increases, the Hero whose triumph every invasion augments; standing on the last sands of life, and encircled by the advancing waters of Darkness and Eternity, it becomes in its expiring effort doubly the Victor and the King!"

Impressed by the fervour of his companion, with a sympathy almost approaching to awe, Lord Ulswater pressed Mordaunt's hand, but offered no reply; and both, excited by the high theme of their conversation, and the thoughts which it produced, moved in silence from their post and walked slowly homeward.

CHAPTER LXXXVII.

> Is it possible?
> Is't so? I can no longer what I would
> No longer draw back at my liking! I
> Must do the deed because I thought of it.
> . . . . . .
> What is thy enterprise, — thy aim, thy object?
> Hast honestly confessed it to thyself?
> O bloody, frightful deed!
> . . . . . .
> Was that my purpose when we parted?
> O God of Justice! — COLERIDGE: Wallenstein.

We need scarcely say that one of the persons overheard by Mr. Brown was Wolfe, and the peculiar tone of oratorical exaggeration, characteristic of the man, has already informed the reader with which of the two he is identified.

On the evening after the conversation — the evening fixed for the desperate design on which he had set the last hazard of his life — the republican, parting from the companions with whom he had passed the day, returned home to compose the fever of his excited thoughts, and have a brief hour of solitary meditation, previous to the committal of that act which he knew must be his immediate passport to the jail and the gibbet. On entering his squalid and miserable home, the woman of the house, a blear-eyed and filthy hag, who was holding to her withered breast an infant, which, even in sucking the stream that nourished its tainted existence, betrayed upon its haggard countenance the polluted nature of the mother's milk, from which it drew at once the support of life and the seeds of death, — this woman, meeting him in the narrow passage, arrested his steps to acquaint him that a gentleman had that day called upon him and left a letter in his room with strict charge of care and speed in its delivery. The visitor had not, however, communicated his name, though the curiosity excited by his mien and dress had prompted the crone particularly to demand it.

Little affected by this incident, which to the hostess seemed no unimportant event, Wolfe pushed the woman aside with an impatient gesture, and, scarcely conscious of the abuse which followed this motion, hastened up the sordid stairs to his apartment. He sat himself down upon the foot of his bed, and, covering his face with his hands, surrendered his mind to the tide of contending emotions which rushed upon it.

What was he about to commit? Murder!—murder in its coldest and most premeditated guise! "No!" cried he aloud, starting from the bed, and dashing his clenched hand violently against his brow, "no! no! no! it is not murder: it is justice! Did not they, the hirelings of Oppression, ride over their crushed and shrieking countrymen, with drawn blades and murderous hands? Was I not among them at the hour? Did I not with these eyes see the sword uplifted and the smiter strike? Were not my ears filled with the groans of their victims and the savage yells of the trampling dastards?—yells which rang in triumph over women and babes and weaponless men! And shall there be no vengeance? Yes, it shall fall, not upon the tools, but the master; not upon the slaves, but the despot. Yet," said he, suddenly pausing, as his voice sank into a whisper, "assassination!—in another hour perhaps; a deed irrevocable; a seal set upon two souls,—the victim's and the judge's! Fetters and the felon's cord before me! the shouting mob! the stigma!—no, no, it will not be the stigma; the gratitude, rather, of future times, when motives will be appreciated and party hushed! Have I not wrestled with wrong from my birth? have I not rejected all offers from the men of an impious power? have I made a moment's truce with the poor man's foe? have I not thrice purchased free principles with an imprisoned frame? have I not bartered my substance, and my hopes, and the pleasures of this world for my unmoving, unswerving faith in the Great Cause? am I not about to crown all by one blow,—one lightning blow, destroying at once myself and a criminal too mighty for the law? and shall not history do justice to this devotedness,—this absence from all self, hereafter—and admire, even if it condemn?"

Buoying himself with these reflections, and exciting the jaded current of his designs once more into an unnatural impetus, the unhappy man ceased and paced with rapid steps the narrow limits of his chamber; his eye fell upon something bright, which glittered amidst the darkening shadows of the evening. At that sight his heart stood still for a moment: it was the weapon of intended death; he took it up, and as he surveyed the shining barrel, and felt the lock, a more settled sternness gathered at once over his fierce features and stubborn heart. The pistol had been bought and prepared for the purpose with the utmost nicety, not only for use but show; nor is it unfrequent to find in such instances of premeditated ferocity in design a fearful kind of coxcombry lavished upon the means.

Striking a light, Wolfe reseated himself deliberately, and began with the utmost care to load the pistol; that scene would not have been an unworthy sketch for those painters who possess the power of giving to the low a force almost approaching to grandeur, and of augmenting the terrible by a mixture of the ludicrous. The sordid chamber, the damp walls, the high window, in which a handful of discoloured paper supplied the absence of many a pane; the single table of rough oak, the rush-bottomed and broken chair, the hearth unconscious of a fire, over which a mean bust of Milton held its tutelary sway; while the dull rushlight streamed dimly upon the swarthy and strong countenance of Wolfe, intent upon his work, — a countenance in which the deliberate calmness that had succeeded the late struggle of feeling had in it a mingled power of energy and haggardness of languor, — the one of the desperate design, the other of the exhausted body; while in the knit brow, and the iron lines, and even in the settled ferocity of expression, there was yet something above the stamp of the vulgar ruffian, — something eloquent of the motive no less than the deed, and significant of that not ignoble perversity of mind which diminished the guilt, yet increased the dreadness of the meditated crime, by mocking it with the name of virtue.

As he had finished his task, and hiding the pistol on his person waited for the hour in which his accomplice was to summon him to the fatal deed, he perceived, close by him on the table, the letter which the woman had spoken of, and which till then, he had, in the excitement of his mind, utterly forgotten. He opened it mechanically; an enclosure fell to the ground. He picked it up; it was a bank-note of considerable amount. The lines in the letter were few, anonymous, and written in a hand evidently disguised. They were calculated peculiarly to touch the republican, and reconcile him to the gift. In them the writer professed to be actuated by no other feeling than admiration for the unbending integrity which had characterized Wolfe's life, and the desire that sincerity in any principles, however they might differ from his own, should not be rewarded only with indigence and ruin.

It is impossible to tell how far, in Wolfe's mind, his own desperate fortunes might insensibly have mingled with the motives which led him to his present design: certain it is that wherever the future is hopeless the mind is easily converted from the rugged to the criminal; and equally certain it is that we are apt to justify to ourselves many offences in a cause where we have made great sacrifices; and, perhaps, if this unexpected assistance had come to Wolfe a short time before, it might, by softening his heart and reconciling him in some measure to fortune, have rendered him less susceptible to the fierce voice of political hatred and the instigation of his associates. Nor can we, who are removed from the temptations of the poor,—temptations to which ours are as breezes which woo to storms which "tumble towers,"— nor can we tell how far the acerbity of want, and the absence of wholesome sleep, and the contempt of the rich, and the rankling memory of better fortunes, or even the mere fierceness which absolute hunger produces in the humours and veins of all that hold nature's life, nor can we tell how far these madden the temper, which is but a minion of the body, and plead in irresistible excuse for the crimes which our wondering virtue—haughty because unsolicited—stamps with its loftiest reprobation!

The cloud fell from Wolfe's brow, and his eye gazed, musingly and rapt, upon vacancy. Steps were heard ascending; the voice of a distant clock tolled with a distinctness which seemed like strokes palpable as well as audible to the senses; and, as the door opened and his accomplice entered, Wolfe muttered, "Too late! too late!"—and first crushing the note in his hands, then tore it into atoms, with a vehemence which astonished his companion, who, however, knew not its value.

"Come," said he, stamping his foot violently upon the floor, as if to conquer by passion all internal relenting, "come, my friend, not another moment is to be lost; let us hasten to our holy deed!"

"I trust," said Wolfe's companion, when they were in the open street, "that we shall not have our trouble in vain; it is a brave night for it! Davidson wanted us to throw grenades into the ministers' carriages, as the best plan; and, faith, we can try that if all else fails!"

Wolfe remained silent: indeed he scarcely heard his companion; for a sullen indifference to all things around him had wrapped his spirit,— that singular feeling, or rather absence from feeling, common to all men, when bound on some exciting action, upon which their minds are already and wholly bent; which renders them utterly without thought, when the superficial would imagine they were the most full of it, and leads them to the threshold of that event which had before engrossed all their most waking and fervid contemplation with a blind and mechanical unconsciousness, resembling the influence of a dream.

They arrived at the place they had selected for their station; sometimes walking to and fro in order to escape observation, sometimes hiding behind the pillars of a neighbouring house, they awaited the coming of their victims. The time passed on; the streets grew more and more empty; and, at last, only the visitation of the watchman or the occasional steps of some homeward wanderer disturbed the solitude of their station.

At last, just after midnight, two men were seen approaching towards them, linked arm in arm, and walking very slowly.

"Hist! hist!" whispered Wolfe's comrade, "there they are at last; is your pistol cocked?"

"Ay," answered Wolfe, "and yours: man, collect yourself your hand shakes."

"It is with the cold then," said the ruffian, using, unconsciously, a celebrated reply; "let us withdraw behind the pillar."

They did so: the figures approached them; the night, though starlit, was not sufficiently clear to give the assassins more than the outline of their shapes and the characters of their height and air.

"Which," said Wolfe, in a whisper,—for, as he had said, he had never seen either of his intended victims,—"which is my prey?"

"Oh, the nearest to you," said the other, with trembling accents; "you know his d—d proud walk, and erect head that is the way he answers the people's petitions, I'll be sworn. The taller and farther one, who stoops more in his gait, is mine."

The strangers were now at hand.

"You know you are to fire first, Wolfe," whispered the nearer ruffian, whose heart had long failed him, and who was already meditating escape.

"But are you sure, quite sure, of the identity of our prey?" said Wolfe, grasping his pistol.

"Yes, yes," said the other; and, indeed, the air of the nearest person approaching them bore, in the distance, a strong resemblance to that of the minister it was supposed to designate. His companion, who appeared much younger and of a mien equally patrician, but far less proud, seemed listening to the supposed minister with the most earnest attention. Apparently occupied with their conversation, when about twenty yards from the assassins they stood still for a few moments.

"Stop, Wolfe, stop," said the republican's accomplice, whose Indian complexion, by fear, and the wan light of the lamps and skies, faded into a jaundiced and yellow hue, while the bony whiteness of his teeth made a grim contrast with the glare of his small, black, sparkling eyes. "Stop, Wolfe, hold your hand. I see, now, that I was mistaken; the farther one is a stranger to me, and the nearer one is much thinner than the minister: pocket your pistol,—quick! quick!—and let us withdraw."

Wolfe dropped his hand, as if dissuaded from his design but as he looked upon the trembling frame and chattering teeth of his terrified accomplice, a sudden, and not unnatural, idea darted across his mind that he was wilfully deceived by the fears of his companion; and that the strangers, who had now resumed their way, were indeed what his accomplice had first reported them to be. Filled with this impression, and acting upon the momentary spur which it gave, the infatuated and fated man pushed aside his comrade, with a muttered oath at his cowardice and treachery, and taking a sure and steady, though quick, aim at the person, who was now just within the certain destruction of his hand, he fired the pistol. The stranger reeled and fell into the arms of his companion.

"Hurrah!" cried the murderer, leaping from his hiding place, and walking with rapid strides towards his victim, "hurrah! for liberty and England!"

Scarce had he uttered those prostituted names, before the triumph of misguided zeal faded suddenly and forever from his brow and soul.

The wounded man leaned back in the supporting arms of his chilled and horror-stricken friend; who, kneeling on one knee to support him, fixed his eager eyes upon the pale and changing countenance of his burden, unconscious of the presence of the assassin.

"Speak, Mordaunt; speak! how is it with you?" he said. Recalled from his torpor by the voice, Mordaunt opened his eyes, and muttering, "My child, my child," sank back again; and Lord Ulswater (for it was he) felt, by his increased weight, that death was hastening rapidly on its victim.

"Oh!" said he, bitterly, and recalling their last conversation—"oh! where, where, when this man—the wise, the kind, the innocent, almost the perfect—falls thus in the very prime of existence, by a sudden blow from an obscure hand, unblest in life, inglorious in death,—oh! where, where is this boasted triumph of Virtue, or where is its reward?"

True to his idol at the last, as these words fell upon his dizzy and receding senses, Mordaunt raised himself by a sudden though momentary exertion, and, fixing his eyes full upon Lord Ulswater, his moving lips (for his voice was already gone) seemed to shape out the answer, "It is here!"

With this last effort, and with an expression upon his aspect which seemed at once to soften and to hallow the haughty and calm character which in life it was wont to bear, Algernon Mordaunt fell once more back into the arms of his companion and immediately expired.

CHAPTER LXXXVIII.

Come, Death, these are thy victims, and the axe
Waits those who claimed the chariot.—Thus we count
Our treasures in the dark, and when the light
Breaks on the cheated eye, we find the coin
Was skulls—

  . . . . . .
              Yet the while
Fate links strange contrasts, and the scaffold's gloom
Is neighboured by the altar.—ANONYMOUS.

When Crauford's guilt and imprisonment became known; when inquiry developed, day after day, some new maze in the mighty and intricate machinery of his sublime dishonesty; when houses of the most reputed wealth and profuse splendour, whose affairs Crauford had transacted, were discovered to have been for years utterly undermined and beggared, and only supported by the extraordinary genius of the individual by whose extraordinary guilt, now no longer concealed, they were suddenly and irretrievably destroyed; when it was ascertained that, for nearly the fifth part of a century, a system of villany had been carried on throughout Europe, in a thousand different relations, without a single breath of suspicion, and yet which a single breath of suspicion could at once have arrested and exposed; when it was proved that a man whose luxury had exceeded the pomp of princes, and whose wealth was supposed more inexhaustible than the enchanted purse of Fortunatus, had for eighteen years been a penniless pensioner upon the prosperity of others; when the long scroll of this almost incredible fraud was slowly, piece by piece, unrolled before the terrified curiosity of his public, an invading army at the Temple gates could scarcely have excited such universal consternation and dismay.

The mob, always the first to execute justice, in their own inimitable way took vengeance upon Crauford by burning the house no longer his, and the houses of his partners, who were the worst and most innocent sufferers for his crime. No epithet of horror and hatred was too severe for the offender; and serious apprehension for the safety of Newgate, his present habitation, was generally expressed. The more saintly members of that sect to which the hypocrite had ostensibly belonged, held up their hands, and declared that the fall of the Pharisee was a judgment of Providence. Nor did they think it worth while to make, for a moment, the trifling inquiry how far the judgment of Providence was also implicated in the destruction of the numerous and innocent families he had ruined!

But, whether from that admiration for genius, common to the vulgar, which forgets all crime in the cleverness of committing it, or from that sagacious disposition peculiar to the English, which makes a hero of any person eminently wicked, no sooner did Crauford's trial come on than the tide of popular feeling experienced a sudden revulsion. It became, in an instant, the fashion to admire and to pity a gentleman so talented and so unfortunate. Likenesses of Mr. Crauford appeared in every print-shop in town; the papers discovered that he was the very fac-simile of the great King of Prussia. The laureate made an ode upon him, which was set to music; and the public learned, with tears of compassionate regret at so romantic a circumstance, that pigeon-pies were sent daily to his prison, made by the delicate hands of one of his former mistresses. Some sensation, also, was excited by the circumstance of his poor wife (who soon afterwards died of a broken heart) coming to him in prison, and being with difficulty torn away; but then, conjugal affection is so very commonplace, and there was something so engrossingly pathetic in the anecdote of the pigeon- pies!

It must be confessed that Crauford displayed singular address and ability upon his trial; and fighting every inch of ground, even to the last, when so strong a phalanx of circumstances appeared against him that no hope of a favourable verdict could for a moment have supported him, he concluded the trial with a speech delivered by himself, so impressive, so powerful, so dignified, yet so impassioned, that the whole audience, hot as they were, dissolved into tears.

Sentence was passed, — Death! But such was the infatuation of the people that every one expected that a pardon, for crime more complicated and extensive than half the "Newgate Calendar" could equal, would of course be obtained. Persons of the highest rank interested themselves in his behalf; and up to the night before his execution, expectations, almost amounting to certainty, were entertained by the criminal, his friends, and the public. On that night was conveyed to Crauford the positive and peremptory assurance that there was no hope. Let us now enter his cell, and be the sole witnesses of his solitude.

Crauford was, as we have seen, a man in some respects of great moral courage, of extraordinary daring in the formation of schemes, of unwavering resolution in supporting them, and of a temper which rather rejoiced in, than shunned, the braving of a distant danger for the sake of an adequate reward. But this courage was supported and fed solely by the self-persuasion of consummate genius, and his profound confidence both in his good fortune and the inexhaustibility of his resources. Physically he was a coward! immediate peril to be confronted by the person, not the mind, had ever appalled him like a child. He had never dared to back a spirited horse. He had been known to remain for days in an obscure ale-house in the country, to which a shower had accidentally driven him, because it had been idly reported that a wild beast had escaped from a caravan and been seen in the vicinity of the inn. No dog had ever been allowed in his household lest it might go mad. In a word, Crauford was one to whom life and sensual enjoyments were everything, — the supreme blessings, the only blessings.

As long as he had the hope, and it was a sanguine hope, of saving life, nothing had disturbed his mind from its serenity. His gayety had never forsaken him; and his cheerfulness and fortitude had been the theme of every one admitted to his presence. But when this hope was abruptly and finally closed; when Death, immediate and unavoidable, — Death, the extinction of existence, the cessation of sense, — stood bare and hideous before him, his genius seemed at once to abandon him to his fate, and the inherent weakness of his nature to gush over every prop and barrier of his art.

No hope!" muttered he, in a voice of the keenest anguish, "no hope; merciful God! none, none? What, I, I, who have shamed kings in luxury, — I to die on the gibbet, among the reeking, gaping, swinish crowd with whom—O God, that I were one of them even! that I were the most loathsome beggar that ever crept forth to taint the air with sores! that I were a toad immured in a stone, sweltering in the atmosphere of its own venom! a snail crawling on these very walls, and tracking his painful path in slime!—anything, anything, but death! And such death! The gallows, the scaffold, the halter, the fingers of the hangman paddling round the neck where the softest caresses have clung and sated. To die, die, die! What, I whose pulse now beats so strongly! whose blood keeps so warm and vigorous a motion! in the very prime of enjoyment and manhood; all life's million paths of pleasure before me,—to die, to swing to the winds, to hang,—ay, ay—to hang! to be cut down, distorted and hideous; to be thrust into the earth with worms; to rot, or—or—or hell! is there a hell?—better that even than annihilation!"

"Fool! fool!—damnable fool that I was" (and in his sudden rage he clenched his own flesh till the nails met in it); "had I but got to France one day sooner! Why don't you save me, save me, you whom I have banqueted and feasted, and lent money to! one word from you might have saved me; I will not die! I don't deserve it! I am innocent! I tell you, Not guilty, my lord,—not guilty! Have you no heart, no consciences? Murder! murder! murder!" and the wretched man sank upon the ground, and tried with his hands to grasp the stone floor, as if to cling to it from some imaginary violence.

Turn we from him to the cell in which another criminal awaits also the awful coming of his latest morrow.

Pale, motionless, silent, with his face bending over his bosom and hands clasped tightly upon his knees, Wolfe sat in his dungeon, and collected his spirit against the approaching consummation of his turbulent and stormy fate. His bitterest punishment had been already past; mysterious Chance, or rather the Power above chance, had denied to him the haughty triumph of self-applause. No sophistry, now, could compare his doom to that of Sidney, or his deed to the act of the avenging Brutus.

Murder—causeless, objectless, universally execrated—rested, and would rest (till oblivion wrapped it) upon his name. It had appeared, too, upon his trial, that he had, in the information he had received, been the mere tool of a spy in the ministers' pay; and that, for weeks before his intended deed, his design had been known, and his conspiracy only not bared to the public eye because political craft awaited a riper opportunity for the disclosure. He had not then merely been the blind dupe of his own passions, but, more humbling still, an instrument in the hands of the very men whom his hatred was sworn to destroy. Not a wreck, not a straw, of the vain glory for which he had forfeited life and risked his soul, could he hug to a sinking heart, and say, "This is my support."

The remorse of gratitude embittered his cup still further. On Mordaunt's person had been discovered a memorandum of the money anonymously inclosed to Wolfe on the day of the murder; and it was couched in words of esteem which melted the fierce heart of the republican into the only tears he had shed since childhood. From that time, a sullen, silent spirit fell upon him. He spoke to none,— heeded none; he made no defence on trial, no complaint of severity, no appeal from judgment. The iron had entered into his soul; but it supported, while it tortured. Even now as we gaze upon his inflexible and dark countenance, no transitory emotion; no natural spasm of sudden fear for the catastrophe of the morrow; no intense and working passions, struggling into calm; no sign of internal hurricanes, rising as it were from the hidden depths, agitate the surface, or betray the secrets of the unfathomable world within. The mute lip; the rigid brow; the downcast eye; a heavy and dread stillness, brooding over every feature,—these are all we behold.

Is it that thought sleeps, locked in the torpor of a senseless and rayless dream; or that an evil incubus weighs upon it, crushing its risings, but deadening not its pangs? Does Memory fly to the green fields and happy home of his childhood, or the lonely studies of his daring and restless youth, or his earliest homage to that Spirit of Freedom which shone bright and still and pure upon the solitary chamber of him who sang of heaven [Milton]; or (dwelling on its last and most fearful object) rolls it only through one tumultuous and convulsive channel,—Despair? Whatever be within the silent and deep heart, pride, or courage, or callousness, or that stubborn firmness, which, once principle, has grown habit, cover all as with a pall; and the strung nerves and the hard endurance of the human flesh sustain what the immortal mind perhaps quails beneath, in its dark retreat, but once dreamed that it would exult to bear.

The fatal hour had come! and, through the long dim passages of the prison, four criminals were led forth to execution. The first was Crauford's associate, Bradley. This man prayed fervently; and, though he was trembling and pale, his mien and aspect bore something of the calmness of resignation.

It has been said that there is no friendship among the wicked. I have examined this maxim closely, and believe it, like most popular proverbs,—false. In wickedness there is peril, and mutual terror is the strongest of ties. At all events, the wicked can, not unoften, excite an attachment in their followers denied to virtue. Habitually courteous, caressing, and familiar, Crauford had, despite his own suspicions of Bradley, really touched the heart of one whom weakness and want, not nature, had gained to vice; and it was not till Crauford's guilt was by other witnesses undeniably proved that Bradley could be tempted to make any confession tending to implicate him.

He now crept close to his former partner, and frequently clasped his hand, and besought him to take courage and to pray. But Crauford's eye was glassy and dim, and his veins seemed filled with water: so numbed and cold and white was his cheek. Fear, in him, had passed its paroxysms, and was now insensibility; it was only when they urged him to pray that a sort of benighted consciousness strayed over his countenance and his ashen lips muttered something which none heard.

After him came the Creole, who had been Wolfe's accomplice. On the night of the murder, he had taken advantage of the general loneliness and the confusion of the few present, and fled. He was found, however, fast asleep in a garret, before morning, by the officers of justice; and, on trial, he had confessed all. This man was in a rapid consumption. The delay of another week would have given to Nature the termination of his life. He, like Bradley, seemed earnest and absorbed in prayer.

Last came Wolfe, his tall, gaunt frame worn by confinement and internal conflict into a gigantic skeleton; his countenance, too, had undergone a withering change; his grizzled hair seemed now to have acquired only the one hoary hue of age; and, though you might trace in his air and eye the sternness, you could no longer detect the fire, of former days. Calm, as on the preceding night, no emotion broke over his dark but not defying features. He rejected, though not irreverently, all aid from the benevolent priest, and seemed to seek in the pride of his own heart a substitute for the resignation of Religion.

"Miserable man!" at last said the good clergyman, in whom zeal overcame kindness, "have you at this awful hour no prayer upon your lips?"

A living light shot then for a moment over Wolfe's eye and brow. "I have!" said he; and raising his clasped hands to Heaven, he continued in the memorable words of Sidney, "Lord, defend Thy own cause, and defend those who defend it! Stir up such as are faint; direct those that are willing; confirm those that waver; give wisdom and integrity to all: order all things so as may most redound to Thine own glory!

"I had once hoped," added Wolfe, sinking in his tone, "I had once hoped that I might with justice have continued that holy prayer; ["Grant that I may die glorifying Thee for all Thy mercies, and that at the last Thou hast permitted me to be singled out as a witness of Thy truth, and even by the confession of my opposers for that OLD CAUSE in which I was from my youth engaged, and for which Thou hast often and wonderfully declared Thyself."—ALGERNON SIDNEY.] but—" he ceased abruptly; the glow passed from his countenance, his lip quivered, and the tears stood in his eyes; and that was the only weakness he betrayed, and those were his last words.

Crauford continued, even while the rope was put round him, mute and unconscious of everything. It was said that his pulse (that of an uncommonly strong and healthy man on the previous day) had become so low and faint that, an hour before his execution, it could not be felt. He and the Creole were the only ones who struggled; Wolfe died, seemingly, without a pang.

From these feverish and fearful scenes, the mind turns, with a feeling of grateful relief, to contemplate the happiness of one whose candid and high nature, and warm affections, Fortune, long be-friending, had at length blessed.

It was on an evening in the earliest flush of returning spring that Lord Ulswater, with his beautiful bride, entered his magnificent domains. It had been his wish and order, in consequence of his brother's untimely death, that no public rejoicings should be made on his marriage: but the good old steward could not persuade himself entirely to enforce obedience to the first order of his new master; and as the carriage drove into the park-gates, crowds on crowds were assembled to welcome and to gaze.

No sooner had they caught a glimpse of their young lord, whose affability and handsome person had endeared him to all who remembered his early days, and of the half-blushing, half-smiling countenance beside him, than their enthusiasm could be no longer restrained. The whole scene rang with shouts of joy; and through an air filled with blessings, and amidst an avenue of happy faces, the bridal pair arrived at their home.

"Ah! Clarence (for so I must still call you)," said Flora, her beautiful eyes streaming with delicious tears, "let us never leave these kind hearts; let us live amongst them, and strive to repay and deserve the blessings which they shower upon us! Is not Benevolence, dearest, better than Ambition?"

"Can it not rather, my own Flora, be Ambition itself?"

CONCLUSION.

So rest you, merry gentlemen.—Monsieur Thomas.

The Author has now only to take his leave of the less important characters whom he has assembled together; and then, all due courtesy to his numerous guests being performed, to retire himself to repose.

First, then, for Mr. Morris Brown: In the second year of Lord Ulswater's marriage, the worthy broker paid Mrs. Minden's nephew a visit, in which he persuaded that gentleman to accept, "as presents," two admirable fire screens, the property of the late Lady Waddilove: the same may be now seen in the housekeeper's room at Borodaile Park by any person willing to satisfy his curiosity and—the housekeeper. Of all further particulars respecting Mr. Morris Brown, history is silent.

In the obituary for 1792, we find the following paragraph:

"Died at his house in Putney, aged seventy-three, Sir Nicholas Copperas, Knt., a gentleman well known on the Exchange for his facetious humour. Several of his bons-mots are still recorded in the Common Council. When residing many years ago in the suburbs of London, this worthy gentleman was accustomed to go from his own house to the Exchange in a coach called 'the Swallow,' that passed his door just at breakfast-time; upon which occasion he was wont wittily to observe to his accomplished spouse, 'And now, Mrs. Copperas, having swallowed in the roll, I will e'en roll in the Swallow!' His whole property is left to Adolphus Copperas, Esq., banker."

And in the next year we discover,—

"Died, on Wednesday last, at her jointure house, Putney, in her sixty- eighth year, the amiable and elegant Lady Copperas, relict of the late Sir Nicholas, Knt."

Mr. Trollolop, having exhausted the whole world of metaphysics, died like Descartes, "in believing he had left nothing unexplained."

Mr. Callythorpe entered the House of Commons at the time of the French Revolution. He distinguished himself by many votes in favour of Mr. Pitt, and one speech which ran thus: "Sir, I believe my right honourable friend who spoke last (Mr. Pitt) designs to ruin the country: but I will support him through all. Honourable Gentlemen may laugh; but I'm a true Briton, and will not serve my friend the less because I scorn to flatter him."

Sir Christopher Findlater lost his life by an accident arising from the upsetting of his carriage, his good heart not having suffered him to part with a drunken coachman.

Mr. Glumford turned miser in his old age; and died of want, and an extravagant son.

Our honest Cole and his wife were always among the most welcome visitors at Lord Ulswater's. In his extreme old age, the ex-king took a journey to Scotland, to see the Author of "The Lay of the Last Minstrel." Nor should we do justice to the chief's critical discernment if we neglected to record that, from the earliest dawn of that great luminary of our age, he predicted its meridian splendour. The eldest son of the gypsy-monarch inherited his father's spirit, and is yet alive, a general, and G.C.B.

Mr. Harrison married Miss Elizabeth, and succeeded to the Golden Fleece.

The Duke of Haverfield and Lord Ulswater continued their friendship through life; and the letters of our dear Flora to her correspondent, Eleanor, did not cease even with that critical and perilous period to all maiden correspondents, — Marriage. If we may judge from the subsequent letters which we have been permitted to see, Eleanor never repented her brilliant nuptials, nor discovered (as the Duchess of — — once said from experience) "that Dukes are as intolerable for husbands as they are delightful for matches."

And Isabel Mordaunt? — Ah! not in these pages shall her history be told even in epitome. Perhaps for some future narrative, her romantic and eventful fate may be reserved. Suffice it for the present, that the childhood of the young heiress passed in the house of Lord Ulswater, whose proudest boast, through a triumphant and prosperous life, was to have been her father's friend; and that as she grew up, she inherited her mother's beauty and gentle heart, and seemed to bear in her deep eyes and melancholy smile some remembrance of the scenes in which her infancy had been passed.

But for Him, the husband and the father, whose trials through this wrong world I have portrayed,—for him let there be neither murmurs at the blindness of Fate, nor sorrow at the darkness of his doom. Better that the lofty and bright spirit should pass away before the petty business of life had bowed it, or the sordid mists of this low earth breathed a shadow on its lustre! Who would have asked that spirit to have struggled on for years in the intrigues, the hopes, the objects of meaner souls? Who would have desired that the heavenward and impatient heart should have grown insured to the chains and toil of this enslaved state, or hardened into the callousness of age? Nor would we claim the vulgar pittance of compassion for a lot which is exalted above regret! Pity is for our weaknesses: to our weaknesses only be it given. It is the aliment of love; it is the wages of ambition; it is the rightful heritage of error! But why should pity be entertained for the soul which never fell? for the courage which never quailed? for the majesty never humbled? for the wisdom which, from the rough things of the common world, raised an empire above earth and destiny? for the stormy life?—it was a triumph! for the early death?—it was immortality!

I have stood beside Mordaunt's tomb: his will had directed that he should sleep not in the vaults of his haughty line; and his last dwelling is surrounded by a green and pleasant spot. The trees shadow it like a temple; and a silver though fitful brook wails with a constant yet not ungrateful dirge at the foot of the hill on which the tomb is placed. I have stood there in those ardent years when our wishes know no boundary and our ambition no curb; yet, even then, I would have changed my wildest vision of romance for that quiet grave, and the dreams of the distant spirit whose relics reposed beneath it.

THE END.

52